ender books from tor teen

other ender books from tor

ORSON
SCOTT
CARD

A WAR OF GIFTS

AN ENDER STORY

TOR
TEEN

A
TOM DOHERTY
ASSOCIATES
BOOK
NEW YORK

A WAR OF GIFTS

Copyright © 2007 by Orson Scott Card

Edited by Beth Meacham

A Tor Teen Book
Published by Tom Doherty Associates
175 Fifth Avenue
New York, NY 10010

www.tor-forge.com

Tor® is a registered trademark of Macmillan Publishing Group, LLC.

The Library of Congress has cataloged the Tor edition as follows:

Card, Orson Scott.
    A war of gifts : an Ender story / Orson Scott Card. — 1st ed.
      p. cm.
    "A Tom Doherty Associates Book."
    ISBN 978-0-7653-1282-2 (hardcover)
    ISBN 978-1-4299-4049-8 (ebook)
    1. Wiggin, Ender (Fictitious character)—Fiction. 2. Christmas stories. I. Title.
    PS3553.A655W37 2007
    813'.54—dc22   2007022041

ISBN 978-0-7653-9829-1 (Tor Teen hardcover)

Our books may be purchased in bulk for promotional, educational, or business use. Please contact your local bookseller or the Macmillan Corporate and Premium Sales Department at 1-800-221-7945, extension 5442, or by email at MacmillanSpecialMarkets@macmillan.com.

First Edition: November 2007
First Tor Teen Edition: November 2017

Printed in the United States of America

0 9 8 7 6 5 4 3 2 1

To Tom Ruby,
who has kept the faith
in and out of Battle School

A WAR OF GIFTS

1

SAINT NICK

Zeck Morgan sat attentively on the front row of the little sanctuary of the Church of the Pure Christ in Eden, North Carolina. He did not fidget, though he had two itches, one on his foot and one on his eyebrow. He knew the eyebrow itch was from a fly that had landed there. The foot itch, too, probably, though he did not look down to see whether anything was crawling there.

He did not look out the windows at the falling snow. He did not glance to left or right, not even to glare at the parents of the crying baby in the row behind him—it was for others to judge whether it was more important for the parents to stay and hear the sermon, or leave and preserve the stillness of the meeting.

Zeck was the minister's son, and he knew his duty.

Reverend Habit Morgan stood at the small pulpit—really an old dictionary stand picked up at a library sale. No doubt the dictionary that had once rested on it had been replaced by a computer, just one more sign of the degradation of the human race, to worship the False God of Tamed Lightning. "They think because they have pulled the lightning from the sky and contained it in their machines they are gods now, or the friends of gods. Do they not know that the only thing written by lightning is fire? Yea, I say unto you, it is the fire of hell, and the gods they have befriended are devils!"

It had been one of Father's best sermons. He gave it when Zeck was three, but Zeck had not forgotten a word of it. Zeck did not forget a word of anything. As soon as he knew what words were, he remembered them.

But he did not tell Father that he remembered. Because when Mother realized that he could repeat whole sermons word for word, she told him, very quietly but very intensely, "This is a great gift that God has given you, Zeck. But you must not show it to anyone, because some might think it comes from Satan."

"Does it?" Zeck had asked. "Come from Satan?"

"Satan does not give good gifts," said Mother. "So it comes from God."

"Then why would anyone think it comes from Satan?"

Her forehead frowned, though her lips kept their smile. Her lips always smiled when she knew anyone was looking. It was her duty as the minister's wife to show that the pure Christian life made one happy.

"Some people are looking so hard to find Satan," she finally said, "that they see him even where he isn't."

Naturally, Zeck remembered this conversation word for word. So it was there in his mind when he was four, and Father said, "There are those who will tell you that a thing is from God, when it's really from the devil."

"Why, Father?"

"They are deceived," said Father, "by their own desire. They wish the world were a better place, so they pretend that polluted things are pure, so they don't have to fear them."

Ever since then, Zeck had balanced these two conversations, for he knew that Mother was warning him about Father, and Father was warning him about Mother.

It was impossible to choose between them. He did not *want* to choose.

Still . . . he never let Father see his perfect memory. It was not a lie, however. If Father ever asked him to repeat a conversation or a sermon or anything at all, Zeck would do it, and honestly, showing that he knew it word for word. But Father did not ask anybody anything, except when he asked God.

Which he had just done. Standing there at the pulpit, glaring out at the congregation, Father said, "What about Santa Claus! Saint *Nick*! Is he the same thing as 'Old Nick'? Does he have anything to do with Christ? Is our worship pure, when we have this 'Old Saint Nick' in our hearts? Is he really *jolly*? Does he laugh because he knows he is leading our children down to hell?"

He glared around the congregation as if waiting for an answer. And finally someone gave the only answer that was appropriate for this point in the sermon:

"Brother Habit, we don't know. Would you ask God and tell us what he says?"

Whereupon Father roared out, "God in heaven! Thou knowest our question! Tell us thine answer! We thy children ask thee for bread, O Father! Do not give us a stone!"

Then he gripped the pulpit—the dictionary stand,

which trembled under his hands—and continued glaring upward. Zeck knew that when Father looked upward like that, he did not see the roof beams or the ceiling above them. He was staring into heaven, demanding that all those hurrying angels get out of his way so his gaze could penetrate all the way to God and *demand* his attention, because it was his right. Ask and it shall be given, God had promised. Knock and it shall be opened! Well, Habit Morgan was knocking and asking, and it was time for God to open and give. God could not break his word—at least not when Habit Morgan was holding him to it.

But God took his own sweet time. Which was why Zeck was sitting there on the front row, with Mother and his three younger siblings beside him, all perched on chairs so wobbly they showed the slightest trace of movement. The other children were young, and their fidgets were forgiven. Zeck was determined to be pure, and his wobbly chair might have been made of stone for all the movement it made.

When Father stared into heaven this long it was a test. Maybe it was a test given by God, or maybe Father had already received his answer—received it perhaps the night before when he was writing this sermon—and so the test was from him. Either way, Zeck would pass this test as he passed all the tests laid before him.

The long minutes dragged. One itch would fade, only to be replaced by another. Father still stared into heaven. Zeck ignored the sweat trickling down his neck.

And behind him, somewhere among the seventy-three members of the congregation who had come today (Zeck hadn't counted them, he had only glanced, but as usual he immediately knew how many there were), someone shifted in his seat. Someone coughed. It was the moment Father—or God—had been waiting for.

Father's voice was only a whisper, but it carried through the room. "How can I hear the voice of the Holy Spirit when I am surrounded by impurity?"

Zeck thought of quoting back to him his own sermon, given two years ago, when Zeck was only just barely four. "Do you think that God cannot make his voice heard no matter what other noise is going on around you? If you are pure, then all the tumult of the world is silence compared to the voice of God." But Zeck knew that to quote this now would bring down the rod of chastisement. Father was not really asking a question. He was pointing out what everyone knew: that in all this congregation, only Habit Morgan was really, truly pure. That's why God's answers came to him, and only to him.

"Saint Nick is a mask!" roared Father. "Saint Nick is the false beard and the false laugh worn by the drunken

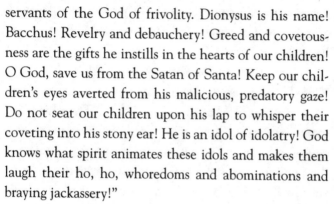

servants of the God of frivolity. Dionysus is his name! Bacchus! Revelry and debauchery! Greed and covetousness are the gifts he instills in the hearts of our children! O God, save us from the Satan of Santa! Keep our children's eyes averted from his malicious, predatory gaze! Do not seat our children upon his lap to whisper their coveting into his stony ear! He is an idol of idolatry! God knows what spirit animates these idols and makes them laugh their ho, ho, whoredoms and abominations and braying jackassery!"

Father was in fine form. And now that he was bellowing the words of God, striding back and forth across the front of the sanctuary, Zeck could scratch the occasional itch, as long as he kept his gaze locked on Father's face.

For an hour Father went on, telling stories of children who put their faith in Santa Claus, and parents who lied to their children about Saint Nick and taught their children that all the stories of Christmas were myths—including the story of the Christ child. Telling stories of children who became atheists when Santa did not bring them the gifts they coveted most.

"Satan is a liar every time! When Santa puts a lie on the lips of parents, the seed of that lie is planted in the hearts of their children and when that seed comes to

17

flower and bears fruit, the fruit of that lie is faithlessness. You do not deserve the trust of your children when you lie for Satan!"

Then his voice fell to a whisper. "Jolly old Saint Nicholas," he hissed. "Lean your ear this way. Don't you tell a single soul what I'm going to say." Then his voice roared out again. "Yes, your children whisper their secret desires to *Satan* and he will answer their prayers, not with the presents they seek, and certainly not with the presence of God Immanuel! No, he will answer their prayers with the ashes of sin in their mouths, with the poison of atheism and unbelief in the plasma of their blood. He will drive out the hemoglobin and replace it with hellish lust!"

And so on. And so on.

In Zeck's mind, the clock that kept perfect time went round the full forty minutes of the sermon. Father never repeated himself once, and yet he also never strayed from the single message. God's message was always brief, Father said, but it took him many words to translate the pure wisdom of the Lord's language into the poor English that mere mortals could understand.

And Father's sermons never ran over. He wrapped them up right in time. He was not a man who talked just to hear himself talk. He labored his labor and then he was done.

At the end of the sermon, there was a hymn and then Father called upon old Brother Verlin and told him that God had seen him today and made his heart pure enough to pray. Verlin rose to his feet weeping and could hardly get out the words of the prayer of blessing on the congregation, he was so moved at being chosen for the first time since he confessed selling an old car of his for nearly twice what it was worth, because the buyer had tempted him by offering even more for it. His sin was forgiven, more or less. That's what it meant, for Brother Habit to call on him to pray.

Then it was done. Zeck leapt to his feet and ran to his father and hugged him, as he always did, for it felt to him when such a sermon ended that some dust of light from heaven must linger still on Father's clothing, and if Zeck could embrace him tightly enough, it might rub off on him, so that he could begin to become pure. Because heaven knew he was not pure *now*.

Father loved him at such times. Father's hands were gentle on his hair, his shoulder, his back; there was no willow rod to draw blood out of his shirt.

"Look, son," said Father. "We have a stranger here in the House of the Lord."

Zeck pulled free to look at the door. Others had noticed the man, too, and stood looking at him, silent until

Habit Morgan declared him to be friend or foe. The stranger wore a uniform, but it wasn't one that Zeck had seen before—not the sheriff or a deputy, not a fireman, not the state police.

"Welcome to the Church of the Pure Christ," said Father. "I'm sorry you didn't arrive for the sermon."

"I listened from outside," said the man. "I didn't want to interrupt."

"Then you did well," said Father, "for you heard the word of God, and yet you listened with humility."

"Are you Reverend Habit Morgan?" asked the man.

"I am," said Father, "except we have no titles among us except Brother and Sister. 'Reverend' suggests that I'm a certified minister, a hireling. No one certified me but God, for only God can teach his pure doctrine, and only God can name his ministers. Nor am I hired, for the servants of God are all equal in his sight, and must all obey the admonition of God to Adam, to earn his bread by the sweat of his face. I farm a plot of ground. I also drive a truck for United Parcel Service."

"Forgive me for using an unwelcome title," said the man. "In my ignorance, I meant only respect."

But Zeck was a keen observer of human beings, and it seemed to him that the man had already known how

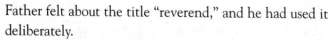

Father felt about the title "reverend," and he had used it deliberately.

This was wrong. This was a pollution of the sanctuary.

Zeck ran from Father to stand a few feet in front of the man.

"If you tell the truth right now," Zeck said boldly, fearing nothing that this man could do to him, "God will forgive you for your lie and the sanctuary will be purified again."

The congregation gasped. Not in surprise or dismay; they assumed that it was God speaking through him at times like this, though Zeck never claimed any such thing. He denied that God ever spoke through him, and beyond that he could not control what they believed.

"What lie was that?" asked the man, amused.

"You know all about us," said Zeck. "You've studied our beliefs. You've studied everything about Father. You know that it's an offense to call him 'reverend.' You did it on purpose, and now you're lying to pretend you meant respect."

"You're correct," said the man, still amused. "But what possible difference does it make?"

"It must have made a difference to you," said Zeck, "or you wouldn't have bothered to lie."

By now Father stood behind him, and his hand on Zeck's head told him he had said enough and it was Father's turn now.

"Out of the mouths of babes," said Father to the stranger. "You've come to us with a lie on your lips, one which even a child could detect. Why are you here, and who sent you?"

"I was sent by the International Fleet, and my purpose is to test this boy to see if he is qualified to attend Battle School."

"We are Christians, sir," said Father. "God will protect us if that is his will. We will lift no hand against our enemy."

"I'm not here to argue theology," said the stranger. "I'm here to carry out the law. There are no exemptions because of the religion of the *parents*."

"What about for the religion of the child?" asked Father.

"Children have no religion," said the stranger. "That's why we take them young—before they have been fully indoctrinated in any ideology."

"So you can indoctrinate them in yours," said Father.

"Exactly," said the man.

Then the man reached out to Zeck. "Come with me,

Zechariah Morgan. We've set up the examination in your parents' house."

Zeck turned his back on the man.

"He does not choose to take your test," said Father.

"And yet," said the man, "he *will* take it, one way or another."

The congregation murmured at that.

The man from the International Fleet looked around at them. "Our responsibility in the International Fleet is to protect the human race from the Formic invaders. We protect the whole human race—even those who don't wish to be protected—and we draw upon the most brilliant minds of the human race and train them for command—even those who do not wish to be trained. What if this boy were the most brilliant of all, the commander that would lead us to victory where no other could succeed? Should everyone else in the human race die, just so you in this congregation can remain . . . *pure?*"

"Yes," said Father. And the congregation echoed him. "Yes. Yes."

"We are the leaven in the loaf," said Father. "We are the salt that must keep its savor, lest the whole earth be destroyed. It is our purity that will persuade God to preserve this wicked generation, not your violence."

The man laughed. "Your purity against our violence." His hand lashed out and he seized Zeck by the collar of his shirt and dragged him sharply backward, toward him. Before anyone could do more than shout in protest, he had torn Zeck's shirt from his body and then whirled him around to show his scarred back, with the freshest wounds still bright red, and the newest of all still beading with blood from this sudden movement. "What about *your* violence? We don't raise our hands against children."

"Don't you?" said Father. "To spare the rod is to spoil the child—God has told us how to make our children pure from the moment they achieve accountability until they have mastered their own discipline. I strike my son's body to teach his spirit to embrace the pure love of Christ. You will teach him to hate his enemies, so that it no longer matters whether his body is living or dead, for his soul will be polluted and God will spit him out of his mouth."

The man threw Zeck's shirt in Father's face. "Come back to your house and you'll find us there with your son, doing what the law requires."

Zeck tore away from the man's grip. The man was holding him very tightly, but Zeck had a great advantage: He didn't care how much it hurt to pull himself free. "I will not go with you," said Zeck.

The man touched a small electronic patch on his

belt and immediately the door burst open and a dozen armed men filed in.

"I will place your father under arrest," said the man from the fleet. "And your mother. And anyone in this congregation who resists me."

Mother came forward then, pushing her way past Father and several others. "Then you know nothing about us," said Mother. "We have no intention of resisting you. When a Roman demands a cloak from us, we give unto him our coat also." She pushed the two older girls toward the man. "Test them all. Test the youngest, too, if you can. She doesn't speak yet, but no doubt you have your ways."

"We'll be back for them, even though the two youngest are illegal. But not till they come of age."

"You can steal our son's body," said Mother. "But you can never steal his heart. Train him all you want. Teach him whatever you want. His heart is pure. He will recite your words back to you but he will never, never believe them. He belongs to the Pure Christ, not to the human race."

Zeck held himself still, so he could not shudder as his body wanted to. Mother's boldness was rare, and always chancy. How would Father react to this? It was *his* place to speak, to act, to protect the family and the church.

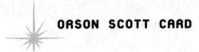

Then again, Father had said several times that a good helpmeet is one who is not afraid to give unwelcome counsel to her husband, and a man so foolish that he can't hear wisdom from his wife is not worthy to be any woman's husband.

"Go with the man, Zeck," said Father. "And answer all questions with pure honesty."

2

ENDER'S
STOCKING

eter Wiggin was supposed to spend
the day at the Greensboro Public
Library, working on a term paper,
but he had lost interest in the
project. It was two days before
Christmas, a holiday that always
depressed him. "Don't get me any
gifts," he said to his parents last
year. "Put the money into mutual
funds and give it to me when I
graduate."

"Christmas drives the American economy," Father said. "We
have to do our part."

"It's not up to you what other
people do and don't give you,"

said Mother. "Invest your own money and don't give *us* gifts."

"Like that's possible," said Peter.

"We don't like your gifts anyway," said Valentine, "so you might as well."

This stung Peter. "There's nothing wrong with my gifts! You sound like I give you used Band-Aids or something."

"Your gifts always look like you bought the cheapest things on sale and then decided after you got them home who you'd give them to."

Which exactly nailed the process Peter went through. "Gee, Valentine," said Peter. "And everyone calls you the *nice* one."

"Can't you two ever stop bickering?" said Mother wistfully.

"Peace on Earth, good will toward brats," said Peter.

That was last year. This year, Peter's investments— anonymous investments, of course, since he was still underage—were doing very well, and he had sold off enough shares to pay for some nice gifts for the family. Nobody was going to say there was anything wrong with *this* year's crop. Though he couldn't spend too much, or Dad would start to get way too curious about where Peter's money was coming from.

His Christmas shopping was done. He wasn't going to do a paper on this topic, and he wasn't ready to start researching another one. There was nothing to do in this miserable town but go home.

Which is why he came into the living room to find Mother crying over—of all things—a Christmas stocking.

"Don't worry, Mother," he said. "You've been good. It won't be coal this year."

She gave him a thin little courtesy laugh and quickly stuffed the stocking back into the box it was stored in. Only then did he realize whose it was.

"Mom," he said. He couldn't help the tone of frustration and reproof in his voice. It's not like Ender was *dead*. He was just in Battle School.

Mom got up from the chair where she was sitting and headed for the kitchen.

"Mom, he's fine."

She turned to him, gazed at him steadily with eyes like fire, though her voice was mild. "Oh—you've had a letter from him? A phone call? A secret report from the school administrators that they didn't provide to Ender's parents?"

"No," said Peter, still unable to keep the impatience from his voice.

Mother smiled acidly. "Then you don't know what you're talking about, do you?"

Peter resented the contempt in her tone. "And stroking his stocking and crying over it, that's supposed to make anything better?"

"You really are a piece of work, Peter," she said, pushing past him.

He followed her into the kitchen. "I bet they hang up stockings for them up in Battle School and fill them with little toy spaceships that make cool shooting noises."

"I'm sure the Muslim and Hindu students will appreciate getting Christmas stockings," said Mother.

"Whatever they do for Christmas, Mother, Ender isn't going to be missing *us*."

"Just because *you* wouldn't miss us doesn't mean *he* doesn't."

He rolled his eyes. "Of course I'd miss you."

Mother said nothing.

"I'm a perfectly normal kid. So's Ender. He'll be busy. He's getting along fine. He's *adapting*. People adapt. To anything."

She turned slowly, reached across and touched his chest, then hooked a finger through the neckline of his shirt and drew him close. "You never adapt," she whispered, "to losing a child."

"It's not like he's dead," said Peter.

"It's exactly like he's dead," said Mother. "I will never

again see the boy who left here. I'll never see him at age seven or nine or eleven. I'll have no memories of him at those ages, only what I can imagine. That's what the parents of dead children have. So until you actually know something about what you're talking about, Peter—human feelings, for instance—why don't you just shut up?"

"Merry Christmas to you too," said Peter. He left the room.

His own bedroom, when he entered it, felt strange to him. Alien. Bare. There was nothing there that expressed a personality. That had been a conscious decision on his part—anything individual that he put on display would give Valentine an advantage in their endless dueling. But at this moment, with Mother's accusation of his inhumanity still ringing in his ears, his bedroom looked so sterile that he hated the person who would choose to live in it.

So he wandered back into the living room and reached into the box of Christmas stockings and pulled out the whole stack. Mother had cross-stitched their names and an iconic picture on each stocking. His own was a spaceship. Ender's stocking had a steam locomotive. But it was Ender in space, the little twit, while Peter was stuck on land with the locomotives.

Peter thrust his hand down into Ender's stocking and

started making it talk like a hand puppet. "I'm Mommy's bestest boy and I've been very very good."

There was something in the toe of the stocking. Peter reached deeper into the sock, found it, and pulled it out. It was just a five-dollar piece—a nickel, as people had taken to calling them, though it was supposedly ten times the value of that long disused coin.

"So you've taken to stealing things out of other people's stockings?" said Mother from the doorway.

Peter felt as embarrassed as if he had been caught in an actual crime. "The toe was heavy," he said. "I was seeing what it was."

"It wasn't yours, whatever it was," said Mother cheerily.

"I wasn't going to keep it," said Peter. Though of course he would have done exactly that, on the assumption that it had been forgotten and would never be missed.

But that was the stocking she had been holding and weeping over. She knew perfectly well the nickel was there.

"You still put stuff in his stocking every year," he said, incredulous.

"Santa fills the stockings," said Mother. "It has nothing to do with me."

Peter shook his head. "Oh, Mother."

"It has nothing to do with you," said Mother. "Mind your business."

"This is *morbid*," said Peter. "Grieving for your hero-boy as if he were dead. He's fine. He's not going to die, he's in the most sterile, oversupervised school in the universe, and after he wins the war he's going to come home amid cheers and confetti and give you a big hug."

"Put back the five dollars," said Mother.

"I will."

"While I'm watching."

That stung. "Don't you trust me, Mother?" asked Peter. He spoke in a sarcastically aggrieved voice, to hide the fact that he really was hurt.

"Not where Ender is concerned," said Mother. "Or me, for that matter. The coin is Ender's. It shouldn't have anybody's fingerprints on it but his."

"And Santa's," said Peter.

"And Santa's."

He dropped the coin down into the sock.

"Now put it away."

"You realize you're making it more and more tempting to set this thing on fire," said Peter.

"And you wonder why I don't trust you."

"And you wonder why I'm hostile and untrustworthy."

"Doesn't it make you just the tiniest bit uncomfortable that I have to wait until I'm sure you're not going to be home before I can allow myself to miss my little boy?"

"You can do what you want, Mother, whenever you want. You're an adult. Adults have all the money and all the freedom."

"You really are the stupidest smart kid in the world," said Mother.

"Again, just for reference, please take note of all the reasons I have to feel loved and respected in my own family."

"I meant that in the nicest, most affectionate way."

"I'm sure you did, Mommy," said Peter. He put the stocking into the box.

Mother came over as he was starting to rise out of the chair. She pushed him back down, then reached into the box and took out Ender's stocking. She reached inside.

Peter took the coin out of his shirt pocket and handed it to her. "Worth a shot, don't you think?"

"You're still so envious of your younger brother that you have to covet everything that's his?"

"It's a fiver," said Peter, "and he isn't going to spend it. I was going to invest it and let it earn him some interest before he gets home in, oh, another six or eight years or whatever."

Mother bent over and kissed his forehead. "Heaven knows why I still love you." Then she dropped the coin into the stocking, put the stocking into the box, reached out and slapped Peter's hand, and then took the box out of the room.

The back of Peter's hand stung from the slap, but it was where her lips had touched his brow that his skin tingled the most.

3

THE DEVIL'S
QUESTIONS

eck got into a hovercar with the man. There was one soldier driving; the rest of the soldiers got into a different vehicle, a larger one that looked dangerous.

"I'm Captain Bridegan," the soldier said.

"I don't care what your name is," said Zeck.

Captain Bridegan said nothing.

Zeck said nothing.

They got to Zeck's house. The door was standing open. A woman was waiting inside, with papers spread out on the kitchen table, along with a pile of blocks and other paraphernalia, including a small machine. She must have noticed Zeck looking at it because she touched it and explained, "It's a recorder. So other people can hear our session and evaluate it later."

Captured lightning, thought Zeck. Just another device used by Satan to snare the souls of men.

"My name," she said, "is Agnes O'Toole."

"He doesn't care," said Bridegan.

Zeck extended his hand. "I'm pleased to meet you, Agnes O'Toole." Didn't Bridegan understand the obligation of kindness and courtesy that all men owed to all women, since women's destiny was to go down into the valley of the shadow of death in order to bring more souls into the world to become purified so they could serve God? What tragic ignorance.

"I'll wait out here," said Bridegan. "If that's all right with Zeck, here."

He seemed to be waiting for an answer.

"I don't care what you do," said Zeck, not bothering to look at him. He was a man of violence, as he had already proven, and so he was hopelessly impure. He had no authority in the eyes of God, and yet he had seized Zeck by the shoulders as if he had a right. Only Father had a duty to purify Zeck's flesh; no other had a right to touch him.

"His father beats him," said Bridegan. And then he left.

Agnes looked at him with raised eyebrows, but Zeck saw no need to explain. They had known about the chastisement of the impure flesh before they came—how else would Bridegan have known to take off his shirt and show the marks? Bridegan and Agnes obviously wanted to use these scars somehow. As if they thought Zeck wanted to be comforted and protected.

From Father? From the instrument chosen by God to raise Zeck to manhood? As well might a man raise his puny hand to prevent God from working his will in the world.

Agnes began the test. Whenever the questions dealt with something Zeck knew about, he answered forthrightly, as his father had commanded him. But half the questions were about things completely outside Zeck's experience. Maybe they were about things on the vids, which Zeck had never watched in his life; maybe they were things from the nets, which Zeck only knew about because they were damnable webs made of lightning, laid before the feet of foolish souls to snare them and drag them down to hell.

Agnes manipulated the blocks and then had him answer questions about them. Zeck saw at once what the purpose of the test was. So he reached over and took the blocks from her. Then he manipulated them to show each and every example drawn on two dimensions on the paper. Except one. "You can't make this one with these blocks," he said.

She put the blocks away.

The next test was entitled "Worldview Diagnostics: Fundamentalist Christian Edition." Since she covered this title almost instantly, it was obvious Zeck wasn't supposed to know what he was being tested on.

She began with questions about the creation and Adam and Eve.

Zeck interrupted her, quoting Father. "The book of Genesis represents the best job that Moses could do, explaining evolution to people who didn't even know the Earth was round."

"You believe in evolution? Then what about Adam as the first man?"

"The name 'Adam' means 'many,'" said Zeck. "There were many males in that troop of primates, when God chose one of them and touched him with his Spirit and put the soul of a man inside. It was Adam who first had language and named the other primates, the ones that looked like him but were not human because God had not given them human souls. Thus it says, 'And Adam gave names to all cattle, and to the fowl of the air, and to every beast of the field; but for Adam there was not found an help meet for him.' What Moses originally wrote was much simpler: 'Adam named all the beasts that were not in the image of God. None of them could speak to him, so he was utterly alone.'"

"You know what God originally wrote?" asked Agnes.

"You think we're fundamentalists," said Zeck. "But we're not. We're Puritans. We know that God can only teach us what we're prepared to understand. The Bible was written by men and women of earlier times, and it holds only as much as they were capable of understanding. We have a greater knowledge of science, and so God can clarify and tell us more. He would be an unloving Father if he insisted on telling us only as much as humans could understand back in the infancy of our species."

She leaned back in her chair. "So then why does your father call electricity 'lightning'?"

"Aren't they the same thing?" asked Zeck, trying to hide his contempt.

"Well, yes, of course, but—"

"So Father calls it 'lightning' to emphasize how dangerous it is, and how ephemeral," said Zeck. "Your word 'electricity' is a lie, convincing you that because it runs through wires and shifts the on-off state of semiconductors, the lightning has been tamed and no longer poses a danger. But God says that it is in your machines that lightning is at its most dangerous, for lightning that strikes you out of the sky can only harm your body, while the lightning that has tamed you and trained you through the machines can steal your soul."

"So God speaks to your father," said Agnes.

"As he speaks to all men and women who purify themselves enough to hear his voice."

"Has God ever spoken to you?"

Zeck shook his head. "I'm not yet pure."

"And that's why your father whips you."

"My father is God's instrument in the purification of his children."

"And you trust your father always to do God's will?"

"My father is the purest man on Earth right now."

"Yet you have never trusted him enough to let him know you have a word-for-word memory."

Her words struck him like a blow. She was absolutely right. Zeck had heeded Mother and never let Father see his unnatural ability. And why? Not because Zeck was afraid. Because *Mother* was afraid. He had taken her faithlessness inside himself as if it were his own, and so Father could not purify him. Could never purify him, because he had been deceiving Father for all these years.

He rose to his feet.

"Where are you going?" asked Agnes.

"To Father."

"To tell him about your phenomenal memory?" she asked pleasantly.

Zeck had no reason to tell her anything, and so he didn't.

Bridegan was waiting in the other room, blocking the door. "No sir," he said. "You're going nowhere."

Zeck went back into the kitchen and sat back down at the table. "You're taking me into space, aren't you," he said.

"Yes, Zeck," she said. "You are one of the best we've ever tested."

"I'll go with you. But I'll never fight for you," he said. "Taking me is a waste of time."

"Never is a long time," she said.

"You think that if you take me far enough from Earth, I'll forget about God."

"Not *forget*," she said. "Perhaps you'll transform your understanding."

"Don't you understand how dangerous I am?" said Zeck.

"We're actually counting on that," she said.

"Not dangerous as a soldier," he said. "If I go with

you, it will be as a teacher. I'll help the other children in your Battle School see that God does not want them to kill their enemies."

"Oh, we're not worried about you converting the other kids," said Agnes.

"You should be," said Zeck. "The word of God has power unto salvation, and no power on earth or in hell can stand against it."

She shook her head. "I might worry," she said. "*If* you were pure. But you're not. So what power will you have to convert anybody?" She piled up the test booklets and stuffed them in the briefcase with the blocks and the recorder. "I have it on tape," she said loudly, for Bridegan to hear. "He said, 'I'll go with you.'"

Bridegan came into the kitchen. "Welcome to Battle School, soldier."

Zeck did not answer. He was still reeling from what she had said. How can I convert anyone, when I'm still impure myself?

"I have to talk to Father," said Zeck.

"Not a chance," said Agnes. "It's the impure Zechariah Morgan that we want. Not the pure one who confessed everything to his father. Besides, we don't have time to wait for another set of lash wounds to heal."

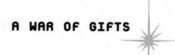

Bridegan laughed harshly. "If that bastard raises his hand against this boy one more time, I'll blast it off."

Zeck whirled on him, filled with rage. "Then what would that make *you?*"

Bridegan only kept on laughing. "It would make me what I've always been—a bloody-minded soldier. My job is defending the helpless against the cruel. That's what we're doing, fighting the Formics—and it's what I'd be doing if I took off your father's hands up to the elbows."

In reply, Zeck recited from the book of Daniel. "'A stone was cut out without hands, which smote the image upon his feet that were of iron and clay, and brake them in pieces.'"

"Without hands. A neat trick," said Bridegan.

"'And the stone that smote the image became a great mountain, and filled the whole earth,'" said Zeck.

"He's got the whole King James version by heart," said Agnes.

"'And in the days of these kings,'" recited Zeck, "'shall the God of heaven set up a kingdom, which shall never be destroyed: and the kingdom shall not be left to other people, but it shall break in pieces and consume all these kingdoms, and it shall stand for ever.'"

"They're going to love him up in Battle School," said Bridegan.

So Zeck spent that Christmas in space, heading up to the station that housed Battle School. He did nothing to cause disturbance, obeyed every order he was given. When his launch group first went into the Battle Room, Zeck learned to fly just like all the others. He even pointed his weapon at targets that were assigned.

It took quite a while before anyone noticed that Zeck never actually hit anybody with his weapon. In every battle, he was zero for zero. Statistically, he was the worst soldier in the history of the school. In vain did the teachers point out that it was just a game.

"'Neither shall they learn war any more,'" quoted Zeck in return. "I will not offend God by learning war." They could take him into space, they could make him wear the uniform, they could force him into the Battle Room, but they couldn't make him shoot.

It took many months, and they still wouldn't send him home, but at least they left him alone. He belonged to an army, he practiced with them, but on every battle report, he was listed with zero effectiveness. There was no soldier in the school prouder of his record.

4

SINTERKLAAS EVE

ink Meeker watched as Ender Wiggin came through the door into Rat Army's barracks. As usual, Rosen was near the entrance, and he immediately launched into his "I Rose de Nose, Jewboy extraordinaire" routine. It was how Rosen wrapped himself in the military reputation of Israel, even though Rosen wasn't Israeli and he also wasn't a particularly good commander.

Not a bad one, either. Rat Army *was* in second place in the standings. But how much of that was Rosen, and how much was the fact that Rosen relied so heavily on Dink's toon—which Dink had trained?

Dink was the better commander, and he knew it—he had been offered Rat Army and Rosen only got it when Dink turned down the promotion. Nobody knew that, of course, except Dink and Colonel Graff and whatever other teachers might have known. There was no reason to tell it—it would only weaken Rosen and also make Dink look like a braggart or a fool, depending on whether people believed his claim. So he made no claim.

This was Rosen's show. Let him write the script.

"*That's* the great Ender Wiggin?" asked Flip. His name was short for Filippus, and, like Dink, he was Dutch. He was also very young and had yet to do anything impressive. It had to gall a young kid like Flip that Ender Wiggin had been placed into the Battle Room early and then rose to the very top of the standings almost instantly.

"I told you," said Dink, "he's number one because his commander wouldn't let him shoot his weapon. So when he finally did it—disobeying his commander, I might add—he got this incredible kill ratio. It's a fluke of how they keep the stats."

"Kuso," said Flip. "If Ender's such a big nothing, why did you go out of your way to get him in your toon?"

So somebody had overheard Dink ask Rosen to assign Ender to his toon, and word had spread. "Because I needed somebody smaller than you," said Dink.

"And you've been watching him. I've seen you. Watching him."

It was easy to forget sometimes that every kid in this place was brilliant. Observant. Clear memory and sharp analytical skills. Even the ones who were still too timid to have done much of anything. Not a good place for doing anything surreptitious.

"É," said Dink. "I think he's got something."

"What's he got that I don't got?"

"Command of English grammar," said Dink.

"Everybody talks like that," said Flip.

"Everybody's a sheep," said Dink. "I'm getting out of here." Moments later, Dink pushed past Rosen and Ender and left the room.

He didn't want to talk to Ender right away. Because this genius kid probably remembered the first time they met. In a bathroom, right after Ender was put in Salamander Army's uniform, his first day in the game. Dink had seen how small he was and said something like, "He's so small he could walk between my legs without touching my balls." It didn't mean anything, and one of his friends had immediately said, "Cause you got none, Dink, that's why," so it's not like Dink had scored any points.

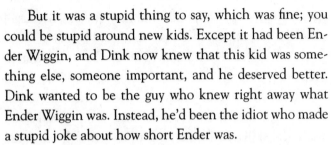

But it was a stupid thing to say, which was fine; you could be stupid around new kids. Except it had been Ender Wiggin, and Dink now knew that this kid was something else, someone important, and he deserved better. Dink wanted to be the guy who knew right away what Ender Wiggin was. Instead, he'd been the idiot who made a stupid joke about how short Ender was.

Short? Ender was small because he was young. It was a mark of brilliance, to be brought to Battle School a year younger than other kids. And then he was advanced to Salamander Army while all the rest of his launch group were still in basic. So he was really under age. And therefore small. So what kind of idiot would mock the kid for being smarter than anybody else?

Oh, suck it up, oomay, he told himself. What does it matter what Wiggin thinks of you? Your job is to train him. To make up for the weeks he wasted in Bonzo Madrid's stupid Salamander Army and help this kid become what he's supposed to become.

Not that Wiggin had really wasted the time. The kid had been running practice sessions for launchies and other rejects during free time, and Dink had come and watched. Wiggin was doing new things. Moves that Dink had never seen before. They had possibilities. So Dink was going to use those techniques in his toon. Give Wiggin a chance to see his ideas played out in combat in the Battle Room.

I'm not Bonzo. I'm not Rosen. Having a soldier under me who's better than I am, smarter, more inventive, doesn't threaten me. I learn from everybody. I help everybody. It's about the only way I can be rebellious in this place—they chose us for our ambition and they prod us to be competitive. So I don't compete. I cooperate.

Dink was sitting in the game room, watching the other players—he had beaten all the games in the room, so he had nothing left to prove—when Wiggin found him. If Wiggin remembered Dink's first dumb joke about his height, Wiggin didn't show it. Instead, Dink let him know which of Rosen's rules and orders he had to obey, and which he didn't. He also let him know that Dink wouldn't be playing power games with him—he was going to get Ender into the battles from the start, pushing him, giving him a chance to learn and grow.

Wiggin clearly understood what Dink was doing for him. He left, satisfied.

There's my contribution to the survival of the human race, thought Dink. I'm not what great commanders are made of. But I know a great commander when I see one, and I can help get him ready. That's good enough for me. I can take this stupid, ineffective school and accomplish something that actually might help us win this war. Something real.

Not this stupid make-believe. Battle School! It was children's games, but structured by adults in order to manipulate the children. But what did it have to do with the real war? You rise to the top of the standings, you beat everybody, and then what? Did you kill a single Bugger? Save a single human life? No. You just go on to the next school and start over as nothing again. Was there any evidence that Battle School accomplished anything?

Sure, the graduates ended up filling important positions throughout the fleet. But then, Battle School only admits kids that are brilliant in the first place, so they would have been command material already. Was there any evidence that Battle School made a *difference*?

I could have been home in Holland, walking by the North Sea. Watching it pound against the shore, trying to wash over and sweep away the dikes, the islands, and cover the land with ocean, as it used to be, before humans started their foolish terraforming experiment.

Dink remembered reading—back on Earth, when he could read what he wanted—the silly claim that the Great Wall of China was the only human artifact that could be seen from space. In fact the claim wasn't even true—at least not from geosynchronous orbit or higher. The wall didn't even cast enough of a shadow to be seen.

No, the human artifact that could be seen from space, that showed up in picture after picture without exciting any comment at all, was Holland. It should have been nothing but barrier islands with wide saltwater sounds behind them. Instead, because the Dutch built their dikes and pumped out the salt water and purified the soil, it was land. Lush, green land—visible from space.

But nobody recognized it as a human artifact. It was just land. It grew plants and fed dairy cattle and held houses and highways, just like any other land. But we did it. We Dutch. And when the sea levels rose, we raised our dikes higher and made them thicker and stronger, and nobody thought, Wow, look at the Dutch, they created the largest human artifact on Earth, and they're *still making it*, a thousand years later.

I could have been home in Holland until they were actually ready to have me do something real. As real as the land behind the dikes.

Free time was over. Dink went to practice. Then he ate with the rest of Rat Army—complete with the ritual of pretending that all their food was rat food. Dink noticed how Wiggin observed and seemed to enjoy the game—but didn't take part. He stayed aloof, watching.

That's something else we have in common.

Something *else*? Why had he thought of it that way? What was the first thing they had in common, that made it so standing aloof was something else?

Oh, that's right. I almost forgot. We're the smartest kids in the room.

Dink silently laughed at himself with perfect scorn. Right, I'm not competitive. I know I'm not the best—but without even thinking about it, I assume that I'm therefore *second* best. What an eemo.

Dink went to the library and studied awhile. He hoped that Petra would come by, but she didn't. Instead of talking to her—the only other kid he knew who shared his contempt for the system—he actually finished his assignments. It was history, so it mattered that he do well.

He got back to the barracks a little early. Maybe he'd sleep. Maybe play some game on his desk. Maybe there'd be somebody in a talkative mood and Dink would have a conversation. No plans. He refused to care.

Flip was there, too. Already getting undressed for bed. But instead of putting his shoes in his locker with the rest of his uniform and his flash suit and the few other possessions a kid could have in Battle School, he had set his shoes down on the floor near the foot of his bed, toes out.

There was something familiar about it.

Flip looked at him and smiled wanly and rolled his eyes. Then he swung up onto his bed and started reading something on his desk, scrolling through what must be homework, because now and then he'd run his finger across some section of the text to highlight it.

The shoes. This was December fifth. It was Sinter-klaas Eve. Flip was Dutch, so of course he had set out his shoes.

Tonight, Sinterklaas—Sint Nikolaas, patron saint of children—would come from his home in Spain, with Black Peter carrying his bag of presents, and listen through the chimneys of the houses throughout Holland, checking to see if children were quarreling or disobedient. If the children were good, then they would knock on the door and, when it was opened, fling candy into the house. Children would rush out the door and find presents left in baskets—or in their shoes, left by the front door.

And Flip had set his shoes out on Sinterklaas Eve.

For some reason, Dink found his eyes clouding with tears. This was stupid. Yes, he missed home—missed his father's house near the strand. But Sinterklaas was for little children, not for him. Not for a child in Battle School.

But Battle School is nothing, right? I should be home. And if I were home, I'd be helping to make Sinterklaas Day for the younger children. If there had been any younger children in our house.

Without really deciding to do it, Dink took out his desk and started to write.

> *His shoes will sit and gather moss*
> *Without a gift from Sinterklaas*
> *For when a soldier cannot cross*
> *The battle room without a loss*
> *Then why should Sinterklaas equip*
> *A kid who cannot fly with zip*
> *But crawls instead just like a drip*
> *Of rain on glass, not like a ship*
> *That flies through space: I speak of Flip.*

It wasn't a great poem, of course, but the whole idea of Sinterklaas poems was that they made fun of the recipient of the gift without giving offense. The lamer the poem, the more it made fun of the giver of the gift rather than the target of the rhyme. Flip still got teased about the fact that when he first was assigned to Rat Army, a couple of times he had bad launches from the wall of Battle Room and ended up floating like a feather across the room, a perfect target for the enemy.

Dink would have written the verse in Dutch, but it was a dying language, and Dink didn't know if he spoke it well enough to actually use it for poem-writing. Nor was he sure Flip could read a Dutch poem, not if there were any unusual words in it. Netherlands was just too close to Britain. The BBC had made the Dutch bilingual; the European Community had made them mostly anglophone.

The poem was done, but there was no way to extrude printed paper from a desk. Ah well, the night was young. Dink put it in the print queue and got up from bed to wander the corridors, desk tucked under his arm. He'd pick up the poem before the printer room closed, and he'd also search for something that might serve as a gift.

In the end he found no gift, but he did add two lines to the poem:

If Piet gives you a gift today,
You'll find it on your breakfast tray.

It's not as if there were a lot of *things* available to the kids in Battle School. Their only games were in their desks or in the game room; their only sport was in the Battle

Room. Desks and uniforms; what else did they need to own?

This bit of paper, thought Dink. That's what he'll have in the morning.

It was dark in the barracks, and most kids were asleep, though a few still worked on their desks, or played some stupid game. Didn't they know the teachers did psychological analysis on them based on the games they played? Maybe they just didn't care. Dink sometimes didn't care either, and played. But not tonight. Tonight he was seriously pissed off. And he didn't even know why.

Yes he did. Flip was getting something from Sinterklaas—and Dink wasn't. He should have. Dad would have made sure he got something from Black Piet's bag. Dink would have hunted all over the house for it on Sinterklaas morning until he finally found it in some perverse hiding place.

I'm homesick. That's all. Isn't that what the stupid counselor told him? You're homesick—get over it. The other kids do, said the counselor.

But they don't, thought Dink. They just hide it. From each other, from themselves.

The remarkable thing about Flip was that tonight he didn't hide it.

Flip was already asleep. Dink folded the paper and slipped it into one of the shoes.

Stupid greedy kid. Leaving out both shoes.

But of course that wasn't it at all. If he had left only one shoe, that would have been proof positive of what he was doing. Someone might have guessed and then Flip would have been mocked mercilessly for being so homesick and childish. So . . . both shoes. Deniability. Not Sinterklaas Day at all—I just left my shoes by the side of my bed.

Dink crawled into his own bed and lay there for a little while, filled with a deep and unaccountable sadness. It wasn't homesickness, not really. It was the fact that Dink was no longer the child; now he was the one who helped Sinterklaas do his job. Of course the old saint couldn't get from Spain to Battle School, not in the ship *he* used. Somebody had to help him out.

Dink was being, not the child, but the dad. He would never be the child again.

5

SINTERKLAAS DAY

eck saw the shoes. He saw Dink put something into the shoe in the darkness, when most kids were asleep. But it meant nothing to him, except that these two Dutch boys were doing something weird.

Zeck wasn't in Dink's toon. He wasn't really in *any* toon. Because nobody wanted him, and it wouldn't matter if they had. Zeck didn't play.

Which made it all the more remarkable that Rat Army was in second place—they won their battles with one less active soldier than anybody else.

At first Rosen had threatened him and tried to take away privileges—even meals—but Zeck simply ignored him, like he ignored other kids who shoved him and jostled him in the corridors. What did he care? Their physical brutality, mild as it might be, showed what kind of people they were—the impurity of their souls—because they rejoiced in violence.

Genesis, chapter six, verse thirteen: "And God said unto Noah, The end of all flesh is come before me; for the earth is filled with violence through them; and, behold, I will destroy them with the earth."

Didn't they understand that it was the violence of the human race that had caused God to send the Buggers to attack the Earth? This became obvious to Zeck as he was forced to watch the vids of the Scouring of China. What could the Buggers represent, except the destroying angel? A flood the first time, and now fire, just as was prophesied.

So the proper response was to forswear violence and become peaceful, rejecting war. Instead, they sacrificed their children to the idolatrous god of war, taking them from their families and thrusting them up here into the hot metal arms of Moloch, where they would be trained to give themselves over entirely to violence.

Jostle me all you want. It will purify me and make you filthier.

Now, though, nobody bothered with Zeck. He was ignored. Not pointedly—if he asked a question, people answered. Scornfully, perhaps, but what was that to Zeck? Scorn was merely pity mingled with hate, and hate was pride mixed with fear. They feared him because he was different, and so they hated him, and so their pity—the touch of godliness that remained in them—was turned to scorn. A virtue made filthy by pride.

By morning he had forgotten all about Flip's shoes and the paper that Dink had put into one of them the night before.

But then he saw Dink step out of the food line with a full tray, and walk back to hand the tray to Flip.

Flip smiled, then laughed and rolled his eyes.

Zeck remembered the shoes then. He walked over and looked at the tray.

It was pancakes this morning, and on the top pancake, everything had been cut away except a big letter "F." Apparently, this had some significance to the two Dutch boys that completely escaped Zeck. But then, a lot of things escaped him. His father had kept him sheltered from the world, and so he did not know many of the things most of the other children knew. He was proud of his ignorance. It was a mark of his purity.

This time, though, there was something about this that seemed wrong to him. As if the letter "F" in the pancake was some kind of conspiracy. What did it stand for? A bad word in Common? That was too easy, and besides, they weren't laughing like that—it wasn't wicked laughter. It was . . . sad laughter.

Sad laughter. It was hard to make sense of it, but Zeck knew that he was right. The F was funny, but it also made them sad.

He asked one of the other boys. "What's with the F Dink carved into Flip's pancake?"

The other kid shrugged. "They're Dutch," he said, as if that accounted for any weirdness about them.

Zeck took that solitary clue—which he had already known, of course—and took it to his desk immediately after breakfast. He searched first for "Netherlands F." Nothing that made sense. Then a few more combinations, but it was "Dutch shoes" that brought him to Sinterklaas Day, December sixth, and all the customs associated with it.

He didn't go to class. He went to Flip's tidily made bed and unmade it till he found, under the sheet and next to the mattress, Dink's poem.

Zeck memorized it, put it back, and remade the

bed—for it would be wrong to put Flip at risk of getting a demerit that he did not deserve. Then he went to Colonel Graff's office.

"I don't remember sending for you," said Colonel Graff.

"You didn't," said Zeck.

"If you have a problem, take it to your counselor. Who's assigned to you?" But Zeck knew at once that it wasn't that Graff couldn't remember the counselor's name—he simply had no idea who Zeck was.

"I'm Zeck Morgan," he said. "I'm a spectator in Rat Army."

"Oh," said Graff, nodding. "You. Have you reconsidered your vow of nonviolence?"

"No sir," said Zeck. "I'm here to ask you a question."

"And you couldn't have asked somebody else?"

"Everybody else was busy," said Zeck. Immediately he repented of the remark, because of course he hadn't even tried anybody else, and he only said this in order to hurt Graff's feelings by implying he was useless and had no work to do. "That was wrong of me to say that," said Zeck, "and I ask your forgiveness."

"What's your question," said Graff impatiently, looking away.

"When you informed me that nonviolence was not

an option here, you said it was because my motive is religious, and there is no religion in Battle School."

"No open observance of religion," said Graff. "Or we'd have classes constantly being interrupted by Muslims praying and every seventh day—not the *same* seventh day, mind you—we'd have Christians and Muslims and Jews celebrating one Sabbath or another. Not to mention the Macumba ritual of sacrificing chickens. Icons and statues of saints and little Buddhas and ancestral shrines and all kinds of other things would clutter up the place. So it's all banned. Period. So please get to class before I have to give you a demerit."

"That was not my question," said Zeck. "I would not have come here to ask you a question whose answer you had already told me."

"Then why did you bring up— Never mind, what's your question?"

"If religious observance is banned, then why does Battle School tolerate the commemoration of the day of Saint Nicholas?"

"We don't," said Graff.

"And yet you did," said Zeck.

"No we didn't."

"It was commemorated."

"Would you please get to the point? Are you lodging

a complaint? Did one of the teachers make some remark?"

"Filippus Rietveld put out his shoes for Saint Nicholas. Dink Meeker put a Sinterklaas poem in the shoe and then gave Flip a pancake carved with the initial 'F.' An edible initial is a traditional treat on Sinterklaas Day. Which is today, December sixth."

Graff sat down and leaned back in his chair. "A Sinterklaas poem?"

Zeck recited it.

Graff smiled and chuckled a little.

"So you think it's funny when they have *their* religious observance, but *my* religious observance is banned."

"It was a poem in a shoe. I give you permission to write all the poems you want and insert them into people's wearing apparel."

"Poems in shoes are not my religious observance. Mine is to contribute a small part to peace on Earth."

"You're not even *on* Earth."

"I would be, if I hadn't been kidnapped and enslaved to the service of Mammon," said Zeck mildly.

You've been here almost a year, thought Graff, and you're still singing the same tune. Doesn't peer pressure have *any* effect on you?

"If these Dutch Christians have their Saint Nicholas

Day, then the Muslims should have Ramadan and the Jews should have the Feast of Tabernacles and I should be able to live the gospel of love and peace."

"Why are you even bothering with this?" said Graff. "The only thing I can do is punish them for a rather sweet gesture. It will make people hate you more."

"You mean you intend to tell them who reported them?"

"No, Zeck. I know how you operate. You'll tell them yourself, so they'll be angry and people will persecute you and that will make you feel more purified."

For a man who didn't recognize him when he came in, Graff certainly knew a lot about him. His face wasn't known, but his ideas were. Zeck's persistence in his faith *was* making an impression.

"If Battle School bans my religion because it forbids all religion, then all religion should *be* forbidden, sir."

"I know that," said Graff. "I also know you're an insufferable twit."

"I believe that remark falls under the topic of 'The commander's responsibility to build morale,' is that correct, sir?" asked Zeck.

"And that remark falls under the category of 'You won't get out of Battle School by being a smartass,'" said Graff.

"Better a smartass than an insufferable twit, sir," said Zeck.

"Get out of my office."

An hour later, Flip and Dink had been called in and reprimanded and the poem confiscated.

"Aren't you going to take his shoes, sir?" asked Dink. "And I'm sure we can recover his initial when he shits it out. I'll reshape it for you so there's no mistaking it, sir."

Graff said nothing, except to send them back to class. He knew that word of this would circulate throughout Battle School. But if he hadn't done it, then Zeck would have made sure that word of how this "religious observance" had been tolerated would spread, and then there really would be a nightmare of kids demanding their holidays.

It was inevitable. The two recusants, Zeck and Dink, both of whom refused to cooperate with the program here, were bound to become allies. Not that they knew they were allied. But in fact they were—they were deliberately stressing the system in order to try to make it collapse.

Well, I won't let you, dear genius children. Because nobody gives a rat's ass about Sinterklaas Day, or about Christian nonviolence. When you go to war—which is

where you've gone, believe it or not, Dink and Zeck—then childish things are put away. In the face of a threat to the survival of the species, all these planetside trivialities are put aside until the crisis passes.

And it has not passed, whatever you little twits might think about it.

6

HOLY WAR

ink left Graff's office seething. "If they can't see the difference between praying eight times a day and putting a poem in a shoe once a year . . ."

"It was a great poem," said Flip.

"It was dumb," said Dink.

"Wasn't that the point? It was a *great* dumb poem. I just feel bad I didn't write one for you."

"I didn't put out my shoes."

Flip sighed. "I'm sorry I did that. I was just feeling homesick. I didn't think anybody would do anything about it."

"Sorry."

"We're both so very very sorry," said Flip. "Except that we're not sorry at all."

"No, we're not," said Dink.

"In fact, it's kind of fun to get in trouble for keeping Sinterklaas Day. Imagine what would happen if we celebrated Christmas."

"Well," said Dink, "we've still got nineteen days."

"Right," said Flip.

By the time they got back to Rat Army barracks, it was obvious that the story was already known. Everybody fell silent when Dink and Flip stood in the doorway.

"Stupid," said Rosen.

"Thanks," said Dink. "That means so much, coming from you."

"Since when did you get religion?" Rosen demanded. "Why make some kind of holy war out of it?"

"It wasn't religious," said Dink. "It was *Dutch*."

"Well, eemo, you be Rat Army now, not Dutch."

"In three months I won't be in Rat Army," said Dink. "But I'll be Dutch until I die."

"Nations don't matter up here," said one of the other boys.

"Religions neither," said another.

"Well it's obvious religion *does* matter," said Flip, "or we wouldn't have been called in and reprimanded for cutting a pancake into an 'F' and writing a funny poem and sticking it in a shoe."

Dink looked down the long corridor, which curved upward toward the end. Zeck, who slept at the very back of the barracks, couldn't even be seen from the door.

"He's not here," said Rosen.

"Who?"

"Zeck," said Rosen. "He came in and told us what he'd done, and then he left."

"Anybody know where he goes when he takes off by himself?" asked Dink.

"Why?" said Rosen. "You planning to slap him around a little? I can't allow that."

"I want to talk to him," said Dink.

"Oh, *talk*," said Rosen.

"When I say talk, I mean talk," said Dink.

"I *don't* want to talk to him," said Flip. "Stupid prig."

"He just wants to get out of Battle School," said Dink.

"If we put it to a vote," said one of the other boys, "he'd be gone in a second. What a waste of space."

"A vote," said Flip. "What a military idea."

"Go stick your finger in a dike," the boy answered.

"So now we're anti-Dutch," said Dink.

"They can't help it if they still believe in Santa Claus," said an American kid.

"Sinterklaas," said Dink. "Lives in Spain, not the North Pole. Has a friend who carries his bag—Black Piet."

"Friend?" said a kid from South Africa. "Black Piet sounds like a slave to me."

Rosen sighed. "It's a relief when Christians are fighting each other instead of slaughtering Jews."

That was when Ender Wiggin joined the discussion for the first time. "Isn't this exactly what the rules are supposed to prevent? People sniping at each other because of religion or nationality?"

"And yet we're doing it anyway," said the American kid.

"Aren't we up here to save the human race?" asked Dink. "Humans have religions and nationalities. And customs. Why can't we be humans too?"

Wiggin didn't answer.

"Makes no sense for us to live like Buggers," said Dink. "*They* don't celebrate Sinterklaas Day, either."

"Part of being human," said Wiggin, "is to massacre each other from time to time. So maybe till we beat the Formics we should try *not* to be so very very human."

"And maybe," said Dink, "soldiers fight for what they care about, and what they care about is their families and their traditions and their faith and their nation—the very stuff they don't allow us to have here."

"Maybe we fight so we can get back home and find all that stuff still there, waiting for us," said Wiggin.

"Maybe none of us are fighting at all," said Flip. "It's not like anything we do here is real."

"I'll tell you what's real," said Dink. "I was Sinterklaas's helper last night." Then he grinned.

"So you're finally admitting you're an elf," said the American kid, grinning back.

"How many Dutch kids are there in Battle School?" said Dink. "Sinterklaas is definitely a minority cultural icon, right? Nothing like Santa Claus, right?"

Rosen kicked Dink lightly on the shin. "What do you think you're doing, Dink?"

"Santa Claus isn't a religious figure, either. Nobody prays to Santa Claus. It's an *American* thing."

"Canadian too," said another kid.

"Anglophone Canadian," said another. "Papa Noël for some of us."

"Father Christmas," said a Brit.

"See? Not Christian, *national*," said Dink. "It's one thing to stifle religious expression. But to try to erase nationality—the whole fleet is thick with national loyalties. They don't make Dutch *admirals* pretend not to be Dutch. They wouldn't stand for it."

"There aren't any Dutch admirals," said the Brit.

It wasn't that Dink let idiotic comments like this make him *angry*. He didn't want to hit anybody. He didn't want to raise his voice. But still, there was this deep defiance that could not be ignored. He had to do something that other people wouldn't like. Even though he knew it would cause trouble and accomplish nothing at all, he was going to do it, and it was going to start right now.

"They were able to stifle our Dutch holiday because there are so few of us," said Dink. "But it's time for us to insist on expressing our national cultures like any other soldiers in the International Fleet. Christmas is a holy day for Christians, but Santa Claus is a secular figure. Nobody prays to Saint Nicholas."

"Little kids do," said the American, but he was laughing.

"Santa Claus, Father Christmas, Papa Noël, Sinterklaas, they may have begun with a Christian feast day, but they're national now, and people with no religion at all still celebrate the holiday. It's the day of gift-giving, right? December twenty-fifth, whether you're a believing Christian or not. They can keep us from being religious, but they can't stop us from giving gifts on Santa Claus day."

Some of them were laughing. Some were thinking.

"You're going to get in such deep doodoo," said one.

"É," said Dink. "But then, that's where I live all the time anyway."

"Don't even try it."

Dink looked up to see who had spoken so angrily.

Zeck.

"I think we already know where you stand," said Dink.

"In the name of Christ I forbid you to bring Satan into this place."

All the smiles disappeared. Everyone fell silent.

"You know, don't you, Zeck," said Dink, "that you just guaranteed that I'll have support for my little Santa Claus movement."

Zeck seemed genuinely frightened. But not of Dink. "Don't bring this curse down on your own heads."

"I don't believe in curses, I only believe in blessings," said Dink. "And I sure as hell don't believe I'll be cursed because I give presents to people in the name of Santa Claus."

Zeck glanced around and seemed to be trying to calm himself. "Religious observances are forbidden for everybody."

"And yet *you* observe your religion all the time," said Dink. "Every time you don't fire your weapon in the Battle Room, you're doing it. So if you oppose our little

Santa Claus revolution, eemo, then we want to see you firing that gun and taking people out. Otherwise you're a flaming hypocrite. A fraud. A pious fake. A liar." Dink was in his face now. Close enough to make some of the other kids uncomfortable.

"Back off, Dink," one of them muttered. Who? Wiggin, of course. Great, a peacemaker. Again, Dink felt defiance swell up inside him.

"What are you going to do?" said Zeck softly. "Hit me? I'm three years younger than you."

"No," said Dink. "I'm going to bless you."

He set his hand in the air just over Zeck's head. As Dink expected, Zeck stood there without flinching. That was what Zeck was best at: taking whatever anybody dished out without even trying to get away.

"I bless you with the spirit of Santa Claus," said Dink. "I bless you with compassion and generosity. With the irresistible impulse to make other people happy. And you know what else? I bless you with the humility to realize that you aren't any better than the rest of us in the eyes of God."

"You know nothing about God," said Zeck.

"I know more than you do," said Dink. "Because I'm not filled with hate."

"Neither am I," said Zeck.

78

"No," murmured another boy. "You're filled with kuso."

"Toguro," said another, laughing.

"I bless you," said Dink, "with love. Believe me, Zeck, it'll be such a shock to you, when you finally feel it, that it might just kill you. Then you can go talk to God yourself and find out where you screwed up."

Dink turned around and faced the bulk of Rat Army. "I don't know about you, but I'm playing Santa Claus this year. We don't own anything up here, so gift-giving isn't exactly easy. Can't get on the nets and order stuff to be shipped up here, all gift-wrapped. But gifts don't have to be toys and stuff. What I gave Flip here, the gift that got us in so much trouble, was a poem."

"Oh how sweet," said the Brit. "A love poem?"

In answer, Flip recited it. Blushing, of course, because the joke was on him. But also loving it—because the joke was on *him*.

Dink could see that a lot of them thought it was cool to have a toon leader write a satirical poem about one of his soldiers. It really *was* a gift.

"And just to prove that we aren't celebrating actual Christmas," said Dink, "let's just give each other whatever gifts we think of on any day at all in December. It can be Hanukkah. It can be . . . hell, it can be Sinterklaas Day, can't it? The day is still young."

"If Dink would give us all a gift," intoned the Jamaican kid, "that would give our hearts a lift."

"Oh how sweet," said the Brit.

"Crazy Tom thinks everything's sweet," said the Canadian, "except for Tom's own mold-covered feet."

Most of them laughed.

"Was that supposed to be a *present?*" said Crazy Tom. "Father Christmas is doing a substandard job this year."

"It would be pleasant to get a present," said Wiggin. Everybody laughed a little. Wiggin went on, "It would be better to get a letter."

Only a few people chuckled at that. Then they were all quiet.

"That's the only gift *I* want," said Wiggin softly. "A letter from home. If you can give me that, I'm with you."

"I can't," said Dink, now just as serious as Wiggin. "They've cut us off from everything. The best I can do is this: At home you know your family's doing Santa stuff. Hanging up stockings, right? You're American, right?"

Wiggin nodded.

"Hang up your stocking this year, Wiggin, and you'll get something in it."

"Coal," said Crazy Tom, the Brit.

"I don't know what it is yet," said Dink, "but it'll be there."

"It won't really be from them," said Wiggin.

"No, it won't," said Dink. "It'll be from Santa Claus." He grinned.

Wiggin shook his head. "Don't do it, Dink," he said. "It's not worth the trouble it'll cause."

"What trouble? It'll build morale."

"We're here to study war," said Wiggin.

Zeck whispered: "Study war no more."

"Are you still here, Zeck?" said Dink, then pointedly turned his back on him. "We're here to build an army, Wiggin. A group of men who work together as one. Not a bunch of kids hammered down by teachers who think they can erase ten thousand years of human history and culture by making a rule."

Wiggin looked away and said, sadly, "Do what you want, Dink."

"I always do," answered Dink.

"The only gift that God respects," said Zeck, "is a broken heart and a contrite spirit."

A lot of kids groaned at that, but Dink gave Zeck one last look. "And when were you ever contrite?"

"Contrition," said Zeck, "is a gift I give to God, not to you." Only then did Zeck walk away, back toward his bed, where he'd be hidden behind the curvature of the barracks room.

7

STOCKINGS

at Army was only a small percentage of the population of Battle School, but word spread quickly. The other armies began picking it up as a joke. Someone would pick up some scrap of leftover food and drop it on someone else's meal tray, saying, "There you are, from Santa with love." And everybody at the table would laugh.

But even as a joke, it was a gift, wasn't it? Santa Claus was giving gifts all over Battle School within days.

It was more than just gifts. It was stockings. Nobody could say who started it, but after a while it seemed that the giving of every gift was accompanied by a stocking. Rolled up, hidden inside something else, but always a stocking. Nobody hung the stocking up in hopes of getting it filled, of course. It was the other way around—the stockings were being given as part of the gift.

And the recipient of the stocking found a way to wear it, whether it fit or not. Dangling from a sleeve. On a foot, but not matched with the other sock. Inside a flash suit. Sticking out of a pocket. Just for a day, the sock was worn, and then it was given back. It was the stocking more than the words now that said, This is from Santa Claus.

The stockings were needed, because what were the gifts? A few were poems, written on paper. Some of them were food scraps. As the days passed, however, more and more of the gifts took the form of favors. Tutoring. Extra practice time in the Battle Room. A bed that was already made when somebody came back from the showers. Showing somebody how to get to a hidden level in one of the video games.

Even when it wasn't a tangible gift, there was the stocking to make it real.

Father was right, thought Zeck. The parents of these children put the lie of Santa in their hearts, and now it bears fruits. Liars, all of them, giving gifts as homage to the Father of Lies. Zeck could hear his father's voice in his memory: "He will answer their prayers with the ashes of sin in their mouths, with the poison of atheism and unbelief in the plasma of their blood." These children were not believers—not in Christ, and not in Santa Claus. They knew they served a lie. If only they could see that when you do charity in the name of Satan it turns to sin. The devil cannot do good.

Zeck tried to go see Colonel Graff, but he was stopped by a Marine in the corridor. "Do you have an appointment with the commandant of Battle School?"

"No, sir," said Zeck.

"Then whatever you have to say, say it to your counselor. Or one of the teachers."

The teachers were no help. Few of them would talk to him anymore. They'd say, "Is this about algebra? No? Then tell it to somebody else, Zeck." The words of Christ had long since worn out their welcome in this place.

The counselor did listen—or at least sat in a room with him while he talked. But it came to nothing.

"So what you're telling me is that the other students are being kind to each other, and you want it stopped."

"They're doing it in the name of Santa Claus."

"What, exactly, has anyone done to you—in the name of Santa Claus?"

ORSON SCOTT CARD

"Nothing to me, personally, but—"

"So you're complaining because they're being kind to other people and *not* to you?"

"Because it's in the name of—"

"Santa Claus, I see. Do you believe in Santa Claus, Zeck?"

"What do you mean?"

"Believe in Santa Claus. Do you think there's really a jolly fat guy in a red suit who brings gifts?"

"No."

"So Santa Claus isn't part of your religion."

"That's exactly my point. It's part of *their* religion."

"I've asked. They say it isn't religion at all. That Santa Claus is merely a cultural figure shared by many of the cultures of Earth."

"It's part of Christmas," insisted Zeck.

"And you don't believe in Christmas."

"Not the way most people celebrate it, no."

"What do you believe in?"

"I believe Jesus Christ was born, probably not in December at all anyway, and he grew up to be the Savior of the world."

"No Santa Claus."

"No."

"So Santa Claus *isn't* part of Christmas."

86

"Of course he's part of Christmas," said Zeck. "For most people."

"Just not for you."

Zeck nodded.

"All right, I'll talk about this to my superiors," said the counselor. "Do you want to know what I think? I think they're going to tell me it's just a fad, and they're going to let it run itself out."

"In other words, they're going to let them keep doing it as long as they want."

"They're children, Zeck. Not many of them are as tenacious as you. They'll lose interest in it and it will go away. Have patience. Patience isn't against your religion, is it?"

"I refuse to take offense at your sarcasm."

"I wasn't being sarcastic."

"I can see that you also are a true son to the Father of Lies." And Zeck got up and left.

"I'm glad you didn't take offense," the counselor called after him.

There would be no recourse to authority, obviously. Not directly, anyway.

Instead, Zeck went to several of the Arab students, pointing out that the authorities were allowing a Christian custom to be openly practiced. From the first few, he heard the standard litany: "Islam has renounced rivalry between religions. What they do is their business."

But Zeck was finally able to get a rise out of a Pakistani kid in Bee Army. Not that Ahmed said anything positive. In fact, he looked completely uninterested, even hostile. Yet Zeck knew that he had struck a nerve. "They say Santa Claus isn't religious. He's national. But in your country, is there any difference? Is Muhammad—"

Ahmed held up one hand and looked away. "It is not for you to say the prophet's name."

"I'm not comparing him to Santa Claus, of course," said Zeck. Though in fact Zeck had heard his father call Muhammad "Satan's imitation of a prophet," which would make Santa and Muhammad pretty well parallel.

"You have said enough," said Ahmed. "I'm done with you."

Zeck knew that Ahmed had gotten along well enough in Battle School. Their home countries were powerless to insist on religious privileges, so the children in Battle School had been granted exemptions from the obligations of Muslims to pray. But what would he do now that the Christians were getting their Santa Claus? Pakistan had been formed as a Muslim country. There was no distinction between what was national and what was Muslim.

It apparently took Ahmed two days to organize things, especially because it was impossible to ascertain at any given time which earthside time zone they were in—or directly above—and therefore what times they should pray. They couldn't even find out what time it was in Mecca and use that schedule.

So Ahmed and other Muslim students apparently worked it out so that they would pray during times when they were not in class, and would continue to use the exemption for those students who were in an actual battle at a prayer time.

The result was a demonstration of piety at breakfast. At first it seemed only a half-dozen Muslims were involved, the students prostrating themselves and facing—not Mecca, which would have been impossible—but to portside, which faced the sun.

But once the praying began, other Muslim students took note and at first a few, then more and more, joined in the praying. Zeck sat at the table, eating without conversation with his supposed comrades in Rat Army. He pretended not to notice or care, but he was delighted. Because Dink grasped the meaning almost at once. The prayer was a Muslim response to Dink's Santa Claus campaign. There was no way the commandant could ignore this.

"So maybe it's a good thing," Dink murmured to Flip, who was sitting next to him.

Zeck knew it was not a good thing. Muslims had renounced terrorism many years ago, after the disastrous Sunni–Shiite war, and had even reconciled with Israel and made common economic cause. But everyone knew how much resentment still seethed within the Muslim world, with many Muslims believing they were treated unfairly by the Hegemony. Everyone knew of the imams and ayatollahs who claimed, loudly, that what was needed was not a secular Hegemony, but a Caliph to unify the world in worship of God. "When we live by Sharia, God will protect us from these monsters. When God sends a warning, we are wise to listen. Instead, we do the opposite, and God will not protect us when we are in rebellion against him."

It was language Zeck understood. Apart from their religious delusions, they had the courage of their faith. They were not afraid to speak up. And they had numbers enough to force people to listen to them. They would be heard by those who had long since stopped even pretending to listen to Zeck.

The next prayer time was at the end of lunch. The Muslims had spread the word, and all those who intended to pray lingered in the mess hall. Zeck had already heard that the same thing happened in the commanders' mess at breakfast, but now most of the Muslim commanders had come into the main mess hall to join their soldiers in prayer.

Colonel Graff came into the mess hall just before the announced time of prayer.

"Religious observance in Battle School is forbidden," he said loudly. "Muslims have been granted an exemption from the requirement of daily prayers. So any Muslim student who insists on a public display of religious rituals will be disciplined, and any commanders or toon leaders who take part will immediately and permanently lose their rank."

Graff had already turned to leave when Ahmed called out, "What about Santa Claus?"

"As far as I know," said Graff, "there is no religious ritual associated with Santa Claus, and Santa Claus has not been sighted here in Battle School."

"Double standard!" shouted Ahmed, and several others echoed him.

Graff ignored him and left the mess hall.

The door had not closed when two dozen Marines came through the door and stationed themselves around the room.

When the time for prayer came, Ahmed and several others immediately prostrated themselves. Marines came to them, forced them to their feet, and handcuffed them. The Marine lieutenant looked around the room. "Anyone else?"

One more soldier lay down to pray; he was also handcuffed. No one else defied them. Five Muslims were taken from the room. Not roughly, but not all that gently, either.

Zeck turned his attention back to his food.

"This makes you happy, doesn't it?" whispered Dink.

Zeck turned a blank face toward him.

"You did this," said Dink softly.

"I'm a Christian. I don't tell Muslims when to pray." Zeck regretted speaking as soon as he finished. He should have remained silent.

"You're not a good liar, Zeck," said Dink. And now he was talking loud enough that the rest of the table could hear. "Don't get me wrong, I think it's one of your best points—you're used to telling the truth, so you never learned the skill of telling lies."

"I don't lie," said Zeck.

"Your words were literally true, I'm sure. Our Muslim friends did not consult you on the timetable. But as an answer to my accusation that you did this, it was such a pathetically obvious lie. A dodge. If you really had nothing to do with it, you wouldn't have needed a dodge. You answered like someone with something to hide."

This time Zeck said nothing.

"You think this will help your chances of getting out of Battle School. Maybe you even think it will disrupt Battle School and hurt the war effort—which makes you a traitor, from one point of view, or a hero of Christianity, from another. But you won't stop this war, and you won't hurt Battle School in the long run. You want to know what you really accomplished? Someday this war will end. If we win, then we'll all go home. The kids in this school are the brightest military minds of our generation. They'll be running things in country after country. Ahmed—someday he'll *be* Pakistan. And you just guaranteed that he will hate the idea of trying to live with non-Muslims in peace. In other words, you just started a war thirty or forty years from now."

"Or ten," said Wiggin.

"Ahmed will still be pretty young in ten years," said Flip, chuckling a little.

Zeck hadn't thought of what this might lead to back on Earth. But what did Dink know? He couldn't predict the future. "I didn't start promoting Santa Claus," said Zeck, meeting Dink's gaze.

"No, you just reported a little private joke between two Dutch kids and made a big deal out of it," said Dink.

93

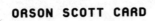

"You made a big deal out of it," said Zeck. "You made it into a cause. You."

Zeck waited.

Dink sighed. "É. I did." He got up from the table.

So did everyone else.

Zeck started to get up too.

Two hands on his shoulders pushed him back down. Hands from two different kids from Rat Army. They weren't rough. They were just firm. Stay here for a while. You're not one of us. Don't come with us.

8

PEACE

The Santa Claus thing was over.
Dink didn't imagine that he controlled it anymore—it had grown
way past him now. But when the
Muslim kids were arrested in the
mess hall, it stopped being a game.
It stopped being just a way to tweak
the nose of authority. There were
real consequences, and as Zeck had
pointed out, they were more Dink's
fault than anyone else's.

So Dink asked all his friends to
ask everybody they knew to stop
doing the stocking thing. To stop
giving gifts that had anything to
do with Santa Claus.

And, within a day, it stopped.

He thought that would be the end of it.

But it wasn't the end. Because of Zeck.

Nothing Zeck did, of course. Zeck was Zeck, completely unchanged. Zeck didn't do anything in practice except fly around, and he didn't do anything in battle except take up space. But he went to class, he did his schoolwork, he turned in his assignments.

And everybody ignored him. They always had. But not like this.

Before, they had ignored him in a kind of tolerant, almost grudgingly respectful way: He's an idiot, but at least he's consistent.

Now they ignored him in a pointed way. They didn't even bother teasing him or jostling him. He just didn't exist. If he tried to speak to anybody, they turned away. Dink saw it, and it made him feel bad. But Zeck had brought it on himself. It's one thing to be an outsider because you're different. It's another thing to get other people in trouble for your own selfish reasons. And that's what Zeck had done. He didn't care about the no-religion rule—he violated it all the time himself. He just used Dink's Sinterklaas present to Flip as a means of making a lame point with the commandant.

So I was childish too, thought Dink. I knew when to stop. He didn't.

Not my fault.

And yet Dink couldn't stop observing him. Just glances. Just . . . noticing. He had read a little bit about primate behavior, as part of the theory of group loyalties. He knew how chimps and baboons that were shut out of their troop behaved, what happened to them. Depression. Self-destruction. Before, Zeck had seemed to thrive on isolation. Now that the isolation was complete, he wasn't thriving anymore.

He looked drawn. He would start walking in some direction and then just stop. Then go again, but slowly. He didn't eat much. Things weren't going well for him.

And if there was one thing Dink knew, it was that the counselors and teachers weren't worth a bucket of hog snot when it came to actually helping a kid with real problems. They had their agenda—what they wanted to make each kid do. But if it was clear the kid wouldn't do it, then they lost interest. The way they had lost interest in Dink. Even if Zeck asked for help, they wouldn't give it. And Zeck wouldn't ask.

Despite knowing how futile it was, Dink tried anyway. He went to Graff and tried to explain what was happening to Zeck.

"Interesting theory," said Graff. "He's being shunned, you think."

"I *know.*"

"But not by you?"

"I've tried to talk to him a couple of times, he shuts me out."

"So he's shunning *you.*"

"But everybody *else* is shunning him."

"Dink," said Graff, "ego te absolvo."

"Whatever you might think," said Dink, "that wasn't Dutch."

"It was Latin. From the Catholic confessional. I absolve you of your sin."

"I'm not Catholic."

"I'm not a priest."

"You don't have the power to absolve anybody from anything."

"But it was worth a try. Go back to your barracks, Dink. Zeck is not your problem."

"Why don't you just send him back home?" asked Dink. "He's never going to be anything in this army. He's a Christian, not a soldier. Why can't you let him go home and be a Christian?"

Graff leaned back in his chair.

"Okay, I know what you're going to say," said Dink.

"You do?"

"The same thing everybody always says. If I let *him* do it, then I have to let everybody else do it."

"Really?"

"If Zeck's noncompliance or whatever it is gets him sent home, then pretty soon you'll have a lot more kids being noncompliant. So they can go home, too."

"Would you be one of those?" asked Graff.

"I think your school is a waste of time," said Dink. "But I believe in the war. I'm not a pacifist, I'm just anti-incompetence."

"But you see, I wasn't going to make that argument," said Graff. "Because I already know the answer. If the only way a kid can go home is acting like Zeck and being treated like Zeck, there's not a kid in this school who'd do it."

"You don't know that."

"But I *do*," said Graff. "Remember, you were all tested and observed. Not just for logic, memory, spatial relationships, verbal ability, but also character attributes. Quick decision-making. Ability to grasp the whole of a situation. The ability to get along well with other people."

"So how the hell did Zeck get here in the first place?"

"Zeck is brilliant at getting along with people," said Graff. "When he wants to."

Dink didn't believe it.

"Zeck can handle even megalomaniacal sociopaths and keep them from harming other people. He's a natural peacemaker in a human community, Dink. It's his best gift."

"That's just kuso," said Dink. "Everybody hated him right from the start."

"Because he wanted you to. He's getting exactly what he wants, right now. Including you coming here to talk to me. All exactly what he wants."

"I don't think so," said Dink.

"That's because you don't know the thing that I was debating with myself about telling you."

"So tell me."

"No," said Graff. "The side arguing for discretion won, and I won't tell."

Dink ignored the obfuscation. Graff wanted him to beg. Instead, Dink thought about what Graff had said about Zeck's abilities. Had Zeck somehow been playing him? Him and everybody else?

"Why?" asked Dink. "Why would he deliberately alienate everybody?"

"Because nobody hated him enough," said Graff. "He needed to be so hated that we gave up on him and sent him home."

"I think you give him credit for more plans than he actually has," said Dink. "He didn't know what would happen."

"I didn't say his plan was conscious. He just wants to go home. He believes he *has* to go home."

"Why?"

"I can't tell you."

"Why not?"

"Because I can't trust you."

"If I say I won't repeat a story, I won't repeat it."

"Oh, I know you can be discreet. I just don't think I can trust you to do the job that needs doing."

"And what job is that?"

"Healing Zeck Morgan."

"I tried. He won't let me near him."

"I know," said Graff. "So the thing you want to know, I'm going to tell to someone else. Someone who is also discreet. Someone who *can* heal him."

Dink thought about that for a few moments.

"Ender Wiggin."

"That's your nominee?" asked Graff.

"No," said Dink. "He's yours. You think he can do anything."

Graff smiled a little Mona Lisa smile, if Mona Lisa had been a pudgy colonel.

"I hope he can," said Dink. "Should I send him to you?"

"I'll bet you," said Graff, "that Ender never needs to come to me at all."

"He'll just know what to do without being told."

"He'll act like Ender Wiggin, and in the process he'll find out what he needs to know from Zeck himself."

"Wiggin doesn't talk to Zeck either."

"You mean that you haven't *seen* him talk to Zeck."

Dink nodded. "Okay, that's what I mean."

"Give him time," said Graff.

Dink got up from his chair.

"I haven't dismissed you, soldier."

Dink stopped and saluted. "Permission to leave your office and return to my barracks to continue feeling like a complete shit, sir."

"Denied," said Graff. "Oh, you can feel like whatever you want, that's not my business. But your effort on behalf of Zeck has been duly noted."

"I didn't come here for a commendation."

"And you're not getting one. All you're getting from

this is my good opinion of your character. It's not easily won, but once won, my good opinion is hard to lose. It's a burden you'll have to carry with you for some time. Learn to live with it. Now get out of here, soldier."

9

WIGGIN

eck came upon Wiggin at one of the elevator wells. It wasn't one much used by students—it was out of the normal lanes of traffic, and mostly teachers used it, when it was used at all. Zeck used it precisely for that reason. He could wait in line at the busier elevators for a long time, but somehow he never got to the front of the line until everyone else had gone. That was usually fine with Zeck, but at mealtime, when everyone was headed for the same destination, it was the difference between a hot meal with a lot of choices and a colder one with almost no choices left.

So there was Wiggin, sitting with his back to the wall, gripping his left leg so tightly that his head rested on his own knee. He was obviously in pain.

Zeck almost walked past him. What did he owe any of these people?

Then he remembered the Samaritan who stopped for the injured man—and the priest and the Levite who didn't.

"Something wrong?" asked Zeck.

"Thinking about something and didn't watch where I was stepping," said Wiggin through gritted teeth.

"Bruise? Broken skin?"

"Twisted ankle," said Wiggin.

"Swollen?"

"I don't know yet," said Wiggin. "When I move it, it throbs."

"Bring your other leg up so I can compare ankles."

Wiggin did. Zeck pulled his shoes and socks off, despite the way Wiggin winced when he moved his left foot. The bare ankles looked exactly alike, as far as he could tell. "Doesn't look swollen."

"Good," said Wiggin. "Then I guess I'm okay." He reached out and grabbed Zeck's upper arm and began to pull himself up.

"I'm not a fire pole," said Zeck. "Let me help you up instead of just grabbing my arm."

"Sure, sorry," said Wiggin.

In a moment, Wiggin was up and wincing as he tried to walk off the injury. "Owie owie owie," he breathed, in a parody of a suffering toddler. Then he gave Zeck a tiny smile. "Thanks."

"Don't mention it," said Zeck. "Now what did you want to talk to me about?"

Wiggin smiled a little more broadly. "I don't know," he said. No attempt to deny that this whole thing had been staged to have an opportunity to talk. "I just know that whatever your plan is, it's working too well or it isn't working at all."

"I don't have a plan," said Zeck. "I just want to go home."

"We all want to go home," said Wiggin. "But we also want other things. Honor. Victory. Save the world. Prove you can do something hard. You don't care about anything except getting out of here, no matter what it costs."

"That's right."

"So, why? And don't tell me you're homesick. We all cried for mommy and daddy our first few nights here, and then we stopped. If there's anybody here tough enough to take a little homesickness, it's you."

"So now you're my counselor? Forget it, Wiggin."

"What are you afraid of?" asked Wiggin.

"Nothing," said Zeck.

"Kuso," said Wiggin.

"Now I'm supposed to pour out my heart to you, is that it? Because you asked what I was afraid of, and that shows me how insightful you are, and I tell you all my deepest fears, and you make me feel better, and then we're lifelong friends and I decide to become a good soldier to please you."

"You don't eat," said Wiggin. "Humans can't live in the kind of isolation you're living in. I think you're going to die. If your body doesn't die, your soul will."

"Forgive me for pointing out the obvious, but you don't believe in souls."

"Forgive me for pointing out the obvious," said Wiggin, "but you don't know squat about what I believe. I have religious parents too."

"Having religious parents says nothing about what you believe."

"But nobody here is religious *without* religious parents," said Wiggin. "Come on, how old were you when they took you? Six? Seven?"

"I hear you were five."

"And now we're so much older. You're eight now?"

"Almost nine."

"But we're so ma*ture*."

"They picked us because we have a mental age much higher than the norm."

"I have religious parents," said Wiggin. "Unfortunately not the same religion, which caused a little conflict. For instance, my mother doesn't believe in infant baptism and my father does, so my father thinks I'm baptized and my mother doesn't."

Zeck winced a little at the idea. "You can't have a strong marriage when the parents don't share the same faith."

"Well, my parents do their best," said Wiggin. "And I bet your parents don't agree on *everything*."

Zeck shrugged.

"I bet they don't agree on *you*."

Zeck turned away. "This is completely none of your business."

"I bet your mother was glad you went into space. To get you away from your father. That's how much they disagree on religion."

Zeck turned around to face him, furious now. "What did those bunducks tell you about me? They have no right."

"Nobody told me anything," said Wiggin. "It's you, oomay. Back when people were still talking to you, when you first came into Rat Army, it was always, Your father this, your father that."

"You only just joined Rat yourself."

"People talk outside their armies," said Wiggin. "And I listen. Always your father. Like your father was some kind of prophet. And I thought, I bet his mother's glad he isn't under his father's influence anymore."

"My mother wants me to respect my father."

"She just doesn't want you to live with him. He beat you, didn't he?"

Zeck shoved Wiggin. Before he even thought of doing it, there was his hand, shoving the kid away.

"Come on," said Wiggin. "You shower. People see the scars. *I've* seen the scars."

"It was purification. There's no way a pagan like you would understand that."

"Purification of what?" asked Wiggin. "You were the perfect son."

"Graff's been feeding you information from their observation of me, hasn't he! That's illegal!"

"Come on, Zeck. I know *you*. If you decide something's right, then that's the thing you'll do, no matter what it costs you. You believe in your father. Whatever he says, you'll do. So what have you done wrong that makes it so you need all this purification?"

Zeck didn't answer. He just closed down. Refused to listen. He let his mind go off somewhere else. To the place where it always went when Father purified him. So he wouldn't scream. So he wouldn't feel anything at all.

"There it is," said Wiggin. "That's the Zeck he made you into. The Zeck who isn't really here. Doesn't really exist."

Zeck heard him without hearing.

"And that's why you have to get home," said Wiggin. "Because without you there, he'll have to find somebody else to purify, won't he? Do you have a brother? A sister? Some other kid in the congregation?"

"He never touched any other kid," murmured Zeck. "I'm the impure one."

"Oh, I know. It's your mother, isn't it? Do you think he'll try to purify your mother?"

At Wiggin's cue, Zeck started thinking about his mother. And not just any picture of her. It was his mother saying to him, "Satan does not give good gifts. So your good gift comes from God."

And then Father, saying, "There are those who will tell you that a thing is from God, when it's really from the devil."

Zeck had asked him why.

"They are deceived by their own desire," Father had

said. "They wish the world were a better place, so they pretend that polluted things are pure, so they don't have to fear them."

He couldn't let Father know what Mother had said, because it was so impure of her. Can't let Father know.

If he whips Mother I'll kill him.

The thought struck him with such force he gasped and stumbled against the wall.

If he whips Mother I'll kill him.

Wiggin was still there, talking. "Zeck, what's wrong?" Wiggin touched him. Touched his arm. The forearm.

Zeck couldn't help himself. He yanked his arm away, but that wasn't enough. He lashed out with his right leg and kicked Wiggin in the shin. Then shoved him backward. Wiggin fell against the wall, then to the floor. He looked helpless. Zeck was so filled with rage at him that he couldn't contain it. It was all the weeks of isolation. It was all his fear for his mother. She really wasn't pure. He should hate her for it. But he loved her. That made him evil. That made him deserve all the purification Father ever gave him—because he loved someone as impure as Mother.

And for some reason, with all of this rage and fear, Zeck threw himself down on Wiggin and pummeled him in the chest and stomach.

"Stop it!" cried Wiggin, trying to turn away from him. "What do you think you're doing, *purifying* me?"

Zeck stopped and looked at his own hands. Looked at Wiggin's body, lying there helpless. The very helplessness of him, his wormlike, fetal pose, infuriated Zeck. He knew from class what this was. It was blood lust. It was the animal fever that took a soldier over and made him strong beyond his strength.

It was what Father must have felt, purifying him. The smaller body, helpless, complete subject to his will. It filled a certain kind of man with rage that had to tear into its prey. That had to inflict pain, break the skin, draw blood and tears and screaming from the victim.

It was something dark and evil. If anything was from Satan, *this* was.

"I thought you were a pacifist," said Wiggin softly.

Zeck could hear his father going on and on about peace, how the servants of God did not go to war.

"'Beat your swords into ploughshares,'" murmured Zeck, echoing his father quoting Micah and Isaiah, as he did all the time.

"Bible quotations," said Wiggin, uncurling himself. Now he lay flat on the ground. Completely open to any blows Zeck might try to land. But the rage was dissipating now. Zeck didn't want to hit him. Or rather, he wanted to hit him, but not more than he wanted *not* to hit him.

"Try this one," said Wiggin. "'Think not that I am come to send peace on earth: I came not to send peace, but a sword.'"

"Don't argue scripture with me," said Zeck. "I know them all."

"But you only believe in the ones your father liked. Why do you think your father always quoted the ones about hating war and rejecting violence, when he beat you the way he did? Sounds like he was trying to talk himself out of what he found in his own heart."

"You don't know my father." Zeck hissed out the words through a tight throat. He could hit this kid again. He could. But he wouldn't. At least he wouldn't if the kid would just shut up.

"I know what I just saw," said Wiggin. "That rage. You weren't pulling your punches. That hurt."

"Sorry," said Zeck. "But shut up now, please."

"Oh, just because it hurt doesn't mean I'm afraid of you. You know one of the reasons I was glad to leave home? Because my brother threatened to kill me, and even though I know he probably didn't mean it, my guts didn't know that. My guts churned all the time. With fear. Because my brother liked to hurt me. I don't think that's your father, though. I think your father *hated* what he did to you. And that's why he preached peace."

"He preached peace because that's what Christ preached," said Zeck. He meant to say it with fervor and intensity. But the words sounded lame even as he said them.

"'The Lord is my strength and song,'" quoted Wiggin. "'And he is become my salvation.'"

"Exodus fifteen," said Zeck. "It's Moses. Old Testament. It doesn't apply."

"'He is my God, and I will prepare him an habitation; my father's God, and I will exalt him.'"

"What are you doing with the King James version anyway?" said Zeck. "Did you learn these scriptures just to argue with me?"

"Yes," said Wiggin. "You know the next verse."

"'The Lord is a man of war,'" said Zeck. "'Jehovah is his name.'"

"The King James version just says 'the Lord,'" said Wiggin.

"But that's what it means when the Bible puts it in small caps like that. They're just avoiding putting down the name of God."

"'The Lord is a man of war,'" said Wiggin. "But if your dad quoted *that*, then he'd have no reason to try to control this bloodlust thing. This berzerker rage. He'd kill you. So it's really a good thing, isn't it, that he ignored Jesus and Moses talking about how God is about war *and* peace. Because he loved you so much that he'd build half his religion up like a wall to keep him from killing you."

"Stay out of my family," whispered Zeck.

"He loved you," said Wiggin. "But you were right to be afraid of him."

"Don't make me hurt you," said Zeck.

"I'm not worried about you," said Wiggin. "You're twice the man your father is. Now that you've seen the violence inside you, you can control it. You won't hit me for telling you the truth."

"Nothing that you've said is true."

"Zeck," said Wiggin. " 'It were better for him that a millstone were hanged about his neck, and he cast into the sea, than that he should offend one of these little ones.' Did your father quote that very much?"

He wanted to kill Wiggin. He also wanted to cry. He didn't do either. "He quoted it all the time."

"And then he took you out and made all those scars on your back."

"I wasn't pure."

"No, *he* wasn't pure. *He* wasn't."

"Some people are looking so hard to find Satan that they see him even where he isn't!" cried Zeck.

"I don't remember that from the Bible."

It wasn't the Bible. It was Mother. He couldn't say that.

"I'm not sure what you're saying," said Wiggin. "That *I'm* finding Satan where he isn't? I don't think so. I think a man who whips a little kid and then blames the kid for it, I think that's exactly where Satan lives."

The urge to cry was apparently going to win. Zeck could hardly get the words out. "I have to go home."

"And do what?" asked Wiggin. "Stand between your mother and father until your father finally loses control and kills you?"

"If that's what it takes!"

"You know my biggest fear?" said Wiggin.

"I don't care about your fear," said Zeck.

"As much as I hate my brother, what I'm afraid of is that I'm just like him."

"I don't hate my father."

"You're terrified of him," said Wiggin, "and you should be. But I think what you're really planning to do when you go home is kill the old son of a bitch."

"No I'm not!" cried Zeck. The rage filled him again, and he couldn't stop himself from lashing out, but at least he aimed his blows at the wall and the floor, not at Wiggin. So it hurt only Zeck's own hands and arms and elbows. Only himself.

"If he laid one hand on your mother—" said Wiggin.

"I'll kill him!" Then Zeck hurled himself backward, threw himself to the floor away from Wiggin and beat on the floor and kept beating on it till the skin of the palm of his left hand broke open and bled. And even then, he only stopped because Wiggin took hold of his wrist. Held it and then put something in his palm and closed Zeck's fist around it.

"You've done enough bleeding," said Wiggin. "In my opinion, anyway."

"Don't tell," whispered Zeck. "Don't tell anybody."

"You haven't done anything wrong," said Wiggin, "except try to get home to protect your mother. Because you know your father is crazy and dangerous."

"Just like me," said Zeck.

"No," said Wiggin. "The opposite of you. Because you controlled it. You stopped yourself from beating the little kid. Even when he deliberately provoked you. Your father couldn't stop himself from beating you—even when you did absolutely nothing wrong at all. You are not alike."

"The rage," said Zeck.

"One of the soldierly virtues," said Wiggin. "Turn it

on the Buggers instead of on yourself or your father. And especially instead of me."

"I don't believe in war."

"Not many soldiers do," said Wiggin. "You could get killed doing that stuff. But you train to fight well, so that when a war does come, you can win and come home and find everything safe."

"There's nothing safe at home."

"I bet that things are fine at home," said Wiggin. "Because, see, with you not there, your mother doesn't have any reason to stay with your father, does she? So I think she's not going to put up with any more crap from him. Don't you think so? She can't be weak. If she were weak, she could never have produced somebody as tough as you. You couldn't have gotten your toughness from your father—he doesn't have much, if he can't even keep himself from doing what he did. So your toughness comes from her, right? She'll leave him if he raises his hand against her. She doesn't have to stay to look out for you anymore."

It was as much the tone of Wiggin's voice as the words he said that calmed him. Zeck pulled his body together, rolled himself up into a sitting position. "I keep expecting to see some teacher rush down the corridor demanding to know what's going on."

"I don't think so," said Wiggin. "I think they know exactly what's going on—probably watching it on a holo somewhere—and maybe they're keeping any other kids from coming along here to see. But they're going to let us work it out on our own."

"Work what out?" said Zeck. "I got no quarrel with you."

"You had a quarrel with everybody who stood between you and going home."

"I still hate this place. I want to get out of here."

"Welcome to the club," said Wiggin. "Look, we're missing lunch. You can do what you want, but I'm going to go eat."

"You still planning to limp on that left ankle?"

"Yes," said Wiggin. "After you kicked me? I won't have to act."

"Chest okay? I didn't break any ribs, did I?"

"You sure have an inflated opinion of your own strength," said Wiggin.

Then he stepped into the elevator and held the bar as it drifted upward, carrying him along with it.

Zeck sat there awhile longer, looking at nothing, thinking about what just happened. He wasn't sure if anything had been decided. Zeck still hated Battle School. And everybody in Battle School hated him. And now he hated his father and didn't believe in his father's phony pacifism. Wiggin had pretty much convinced him that his father was no prophet. Hell, Zeck had known it all along. But believing in his father's spirituality was the only way he could keep himself from hating him and fearing him. The only way he could bear it. Now he didn't have to bear it anymore. Wiggin was right. Mother was free, now that she didn't have to look out for Zeck.

He unclenched his fist and saw what Wiggin had stuffed into it to stanch the bleeding. One of his socks, covered in blood.

10

GRACE

ink saw how Wiggin walked with his food tray and knew something was wrong. And it wasn't just because his tray was double-loaded. Who was he getting lunch for? Didn't matter—what mattered was that Wiggin was in pain. Dink pulled out the chair beside him.

"What happened?" he asked as soon as Wiggin sat down.

"Got lunch for Zeck," said Wiggin.

"I mean what happened to *you*," said Dink.

"Happened?" Wiggin's voice

was all innocence, but his eyes, lasering in at Dink's eyes, were telling him to back off.

"Suit yourself," said Dink. "Keep your dandruff to yourself for all I care."

The conversation at the table flowed around them after that. Dink joined in now and then, but he noticed that Wiggin just ate, and that he was careful about how he breathed. Something had injured his chest. Broken rib? No, more likely a bruise. And he'd been favoring one leg when he walked. Trying not to show it, but favoring it all the same. And he was saving lunch for Zeck. They'd had a fight. The pacifist and the genius? Fighting each other? That was stupid. But what else could it have been? Who else but a pacifist would attack somebody as little as Wiggin?

Half the soldiers were gone from the table by the time Zeck came in. The food line had already closed down, but Wiggin saw him and stood up and waved him over. He was slow raising his hand to wave, though, what with his chest hurting and all.

Zeck approached. "Got lunch for you," said Wiggin, stepping away from his chair so that Zeck could sit in it.

The other kids at the table were obviously poising themselves to leave if Zeck sat down there.

"No, I'm not hungry," said Zeck.

Had he been crying? No. And what was with his hand? He kept it in a fist, but Dink could see that it had been injured. That there had been blood.

"I just wanted to give you something," said Zeck.

He laid a stocking down on the table beside Wiggin's tray.

"Sorry it's wet," said Zeck. "I had to wash it."

"Toguro," said Wiggin. "Now sit and eat." He almost pushed Zeck down into the chair.

It was the stocking that did it. Wiggin had given Zeck a gift—a Santa Claus gift, of all things—and Zeck had accepted it. Now Wiggin stood with his hands on Zeck's shoulders, staring at each of the other Rat Army soldiers in turn, as if he was daring them to stand up and go.

Dink knew that if *he* got up, the others would too. But he didn't get up, and the others stayed.

"So I've got this poem," said Dink. "It really sucks, but sometimes you just gotta say it to get it out of your system."

"We've just eaten, Dink," said Flip. "Couldn't you wait till our food is digested?"

"No, this will be good for you," said Dink. "Your food's turning to shit right now, and this will help."

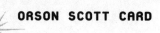

That got him a laugh, which bought him enough time to finish coming up with the rhymes he needed.

> *"What do you do with Zeck?*
> *You want to break his neck.*
> *But I warn you not to try*
> *Cause Zeck's too stubborn to die."*

As poems go, it was pretty weak. But as a symbol of Dink's decision that Zeck should be given another chance, well, it did the job. Between Wiggin's stocking and Dink's poem, Zeck had returned to his previous status: barely tolerated.

Dink looked up at Wiggin, who was still standing behind Zeck—who now seemed to be eating with some appetite.

"Merry Christmas," Dink mouthed silently.

Wiggin smiled.